The Clumsy Tooth Fairy

Lauren Hanson

AN AUTHORS OF THE QUILL BOOK

Contents

Chapter One

ANNA WAS NOT LOOKING forward to today. Just a few minutes ago, her parents received a tree-mail telling them Queen Mary wanted to see her. Queen Mary was the leader of the tooth fairies, and Anna had already seen her once before. It was not fun.

Anna's parents were tooth fairies, as was her older brother. She was still in training since she wasn't old enough to be a full-fledged tooth fairy. Just one more month to go... if she made it that far. Whenever she went on missions with her trainer, no matter what her trainer said about being careful, she always messed up somehow! She would clank the gold coins by accident or trip over toys. The accidents made noise and almost woke up the sleeping children.

Once, she was even cornered by the family cat, who just happened to stay in the child's room at night. Luckily, her trainer spotted a battery-operated mouse and turned it on so the cat would chase it away from her. All these were mistakes that her trainer had to report to the Queen.

Queen Mary would be deciding her fate in a month. She would either become a tooth fairy like her whole family or be given another job where she might not mess things up. *Why can't I be graceful like my mother? Why can't I be as quiet as my father? I would even take being confident like my brother if I could. Anything but being Clumsy Anna!*

She wasn't as clumsy at home as on missions, probably because she knew her house inside and out while the children's homes were all different. Those differences were challenging for her.

She looked at herself in the mirror. If she had to see the Queen, she had to make sure she *looked* perfect, at least. Her hair was pulled back, not a single black hair out of place. Her wings were sparkling clean, with no specks of dust. Lastly, her pink and red outfit remained wrinkle-free. In their community, a fairy only wore clothes that matched their wings. The Queen had made that rule to be sure no one wore colors that looked bad on them.

Anna took the spiral staircase to their tree home's lower living room area. When her family saw her, they all went to her for a group hug. They were hoping to give her comfort before her meeting, but Anna became more nervous. They would only feel like she needed a hug if it was bad news, right?

She stepped back from her family and said, “I will see you later.” They all responded with, “Love you!” Anna tried to smile before turning around and flying out their door. She knew if she stood there too long, she would get more nervous and not want to leave. So, she quickly flew towards the Queen’s willow tree in the center of the glade before she could think about it anymore. She let the wind blow across her face as if it was blowing away her doubts.

As she got closer to the willow, Anna flew lower and landed at the bottom of the tree on the small wooden steps. There was a guard outside the door. "Do you have an appointment?"

"I was sent a request letter from Queen Mary. It did not say a time, so I came quickly."

He nodded and wrote a note in his small notebook. "You may fly up to the third window. Her Majesty is in the throne room."

Anna hurried to follow his instructions and flew up the tree.

Chapter Two

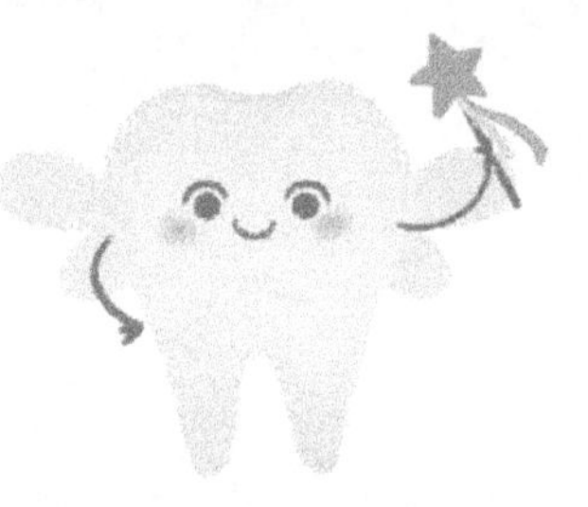

Arriving at the third window, Anna landed on the perch outside and gave a gentle knock. Another guard opened the door that held the window and waved her inside. The throne room was huge! It was the entire width of the tree trunk and big enough to house most of their community if an emergency meeting was called. Right now, it was only the Queen, her assistant, the guard, and Anna.

Anna walked quickly, but quietly, to move closer to the Queen. If she tried talking to her from the door, their voices would echo and words would get confusing. No one needed that headache.

Queen Mary sat on her throne made out of her willow tree's own weeping branches, with the leaves woven throughout adding cushioning. She wore her silver crown with small sapphires all around it, matching her hair's silver and blue tints. Just as Anna had to wear a matching outfit, the Queen did. Her flowing dress of blues and purples perfectly matched the colors of her wings and crown. She embodied poise and grace while still looking stern.

Queen Mary

Once Anna was at the steps leading up to the throne, she bent into a curtsey and waited for the Queen to acknowledge her presence.

"Please rise," Queen Mary said. "Thank you for coming quickly, Anna.

We must discuss your training and next month's initiation."

"Yes, my Queen," Anna responded softly. She was nervous and surprised that any words came out.

"You haven't had the best luck with your tooth fairy training. Have you considered any other paths?"

"No, my Queen. I haven't. My whole family has been tooth fairies, and I don't want to let them down," Anna confessed.

"If you can't find a way to deliver the coins to the children in exchange for their teeth within the next three weeks, you will need to look at other options," Queen Mary informed her.

Anna lowered her head in a bow. It was more to hide her tears than to give respect to her queen. Taking a deep breath to steady her voice, she responded, "Yes, my Queen. I understand."

The queen gave a small wave of her hand and said, "You are dismissed for now."

That was it. Anna wasn't going to try changing her mind because she knew it would not work. She quickly walked over to the window door and the guard opened it for her. She didn't slow down. Anna walked through the door, and when she got to the perch, she flew off.

She knew that if she went home, her family would ask how the meeting went, and she didn't feel able to tell them yet without crying. Instead, she flew off to her secret spot. There was a fairy ring of mushrooms near their glade's stream. Whenever she wanted a quiet and relaxing spot, that is where she went. It didn't take long to get there, and she soon settled upon her favorite mushroom cap. It was red with white spots and reminded her of a strawberry, her favorite food.

She wrapped her arms around her legs and began to think. *How can I be less clumsy?* she thought to herself.

She jumped when a boy fairy's voice responded, "You need to be confident in yourself." She must have spoken aloud without meaning to. She looked across the fairy ring to see a blue and green boy fairy sitting on a dark blue mushroom. "Sorry," he said. "You probably wanted to be alone. I just love this spot and needed a rest."

Chapter Three

"It's okay," Anna told him. "I come here to think and get away from others sometimes."

"If you don't mind, why do you need to be less clumsy anyway?" he asked with a look of confusion on his face.

"If I can't stop making mistakes in tooth fairy training, I will disappoint my family and fail to join their legacy."

"My name is Jax. My family members are gardener fairies. I will be one soon too. We grow the food for the whole glade," he said with pride. "I wouldn't know what else I would do if I weren't gardening. If you don't pass the tooth fairy training, maybe you could try gardening?" he offered.

"I hope it doesn't come to that, but if it does, I am grateful for your invitation."

"You know... Maybe you are trying too hard to be a tooth fairy."

"How so?" she asked. How could one try too hard and still not succeed? She had no idea.

"Well, you said your whole family has always been tooth fairies. I'm sure your trainer is one as well. Sometimes everyone gets so wrapped up in following traditions that they don't listen to themselves. Humans haven't done things in the exact same ways over the years, so why must we? Maybe you need to figure out your own way.

My family used to carry heavy buckets of water around to water the plants. I showed them how to use reeds with holes in them to water the garden like a human uses those soaker hoses. It is faster and less exhausting. You and I? We are the next generation of fairies. Be creative!" Then, he flew off before Anna could respond.

He does have a point, she thought. *How can a tooth fairy be creative, though? We only take teeth and put coins in their places under pillows. What can be creative about that?* Good thing Anna was already in her thinking place. Jax may have just saved her future. If she could figure out how to use his advice, that is.

Jax mentioned how humans have changed, and he was right. Children used to go to bed when the sun went down and played outside all day. Now with electricity, they sometimes didn't fall asleep until quite late and were often found looking at screens with moving pictures. There were times when Anna had arrived at a house only to find the child still awake. Her trainer would make her sit on the tree branch outside their window to watch and wait for them to fall asleep.

Some nights it took them three hours to go to bed! That's a long time, and she would easily doze off unless the humans had a larger screen with a window open. Then she could watch and listen while waiting. Watching the shows helped her learn about humans. She knew most shows were fake, but some things she could use.

What have I noticed that I can use to my own advantage? Hmm. Children love magic and surprises. What would they think if their tooth fairy made up a game?

Anna knew her main issue was staying balanced while taking the coins out of her bag. Making them grow in size from fairy to human coins caused the coins to become big and heavy. They were so big that Anna would stumble, and the coins would fall. It made so much noise! She wondered if she could use her magic differently, relying on things she did at home while in the children's homes. At home, she could float things across the room and catch them. She could also shrink or make them bigger even if they weren't in her hand.

What if I...? What if it's too unusual for the Queen? What if...?

Chapter Four

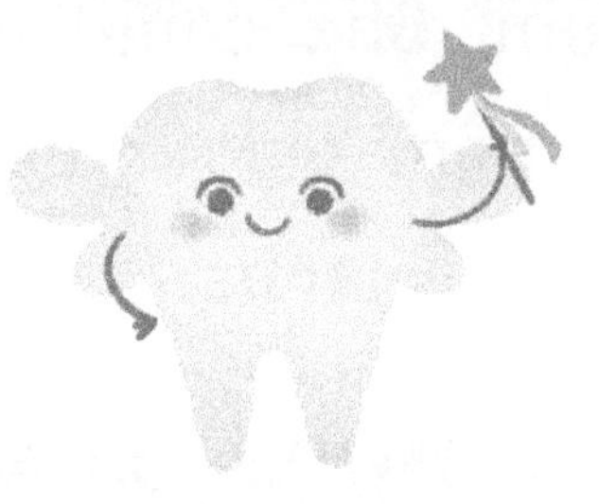

ANNA WOKE UP THE next day ready to learn and excited to start her plan. She was willing to do anything that might save her future as a tooth fairy. She was on the training schedule tonight and already knew who her assignment was. A young girl named Charlotte lost her tooth while brushing her teeth earlier that morning. Charlotte just happened to live within Anna's training area, so she found out much earlier than usual who her child was.

While her family went to socialize in the glade with the other fairies until they had to work, Anna was already flying off to learn about Charlotte. If she wanted her idea to work, she needed to know the girl's routine. It had only been thirty minutes since the girl lost her tooth. Anna watched as she finished breakfast, smiling the entire time with a hole where the tooth used to be. Charlotte carried her empty bowl to the sink before quickly feeding her orange tabby cat some food from a bin. Then she put her unicorn sneakers on and grabbed her sparkly pink school bag.

Charlotte's mom opened the door and hugged her goodbye. The girl walked down the sidewalk and then got on a bus that had just arrived. They really had their routine down! Anna was amazed. She stayed in the tree outside the house for a while, watching what the mother did after her child went to school. Most of the time, her mom was cleaning around the house while watching people on the big screen.

Deciding she had enough information to start her plan, Anna flew back home. She went straight to her room. Anna spent the entire afternoon practicing her magic skills. She could do magic with just her hands, but she practiced with her favorite alder wand. Alder wood was known to be best for magic that didn't need words, just concentration. With her clumsiness, the wand helped focus and direct her magic. It made her plan less risky, or at least she hoped it would.

She began to practice floating different items around her room, from the lightest feather to her heavy wardrobe. She wanted to practice with all weights and sizes to be ready for anything. Once she felt like she could do the floating well enough, she started making items disappear and reappear in different spots. She practiced more on pebbles, feathers, and acorns because she wouldn't miss them if they disappeared forever. In fact, she did lose the first three pebbles and an acorn before she began to succeed at bringing them back.

Anna felt those two magics were going to be the hardest to learn. She managed to get a handle on them just in time to have supper with her family. Sitting at the table, she couldn't avoid their questions about her visit with Queen Mary. She kept her answers simple so she wouldn't accidentally tell them what she was up to. "The Queen wanted to remind me that I have a month to go until my initiation." "She just wanted to know how I felt my training was going." "No, she was quite nice." She ate faster than usual so she could talk less and get back to her room.

Anna still had at least one last trick to practice before she could attempt anything tonight. She found her bag that held coins and would, hopefully, hold a tooth later. The coins were divided into bunches of five. Each bunch was in a shiny, see-through drawstring bag. She remembered the humans calling them organza bags. Right now, they were able to fit into her tiny hand and were light enough that she could fly with them. Since her room was small, she couldn't grow them to full size, but at least she could practice making the coins and bag the size of a pebble, then shrinking them back down.

Soon she was confident in her abilities, and didn't Jax tell her she needed to be more confident to be less clumsy? *Please, Gods of the Glade, please let this plan work,* she pleaded. The next part would be the hardest. Getting her trainer to let her try things her own way...

Chapter Five

SHE WAS ALREADY SITTING in the tree outside Charlotte's home when her trainer fluttered down beside her. Jade took after her name, wearing shades of green and black to match her wings. Anna had never noticed how much that helped Jade camouflage with the trees. Her own pinks and purples stood out if she didn't hide behind a leaf.

"How did your meeting with the Queen go?" Jade asked. Jade was never one to hide her thoughts and always cut to the chase. She also rarely said hello.

Trainer Jade

"It went," Anna answered. "I have a month to go to figure things out." Now for her to see if Jade would let her try out her idea. *How much do I tell her?* "I have a new idea. I know you want me to follow tradition but, with my clumsiness, it doesn't work. I want to test out something new. That is if you can give me the time I have left to see if my plan will work?"

Jade sat down on the branch, hand under her chin, to think. "I don't know what you are thinking, but if you believe it will work, I will just stand by and watch in case I'm needed."

Anna smiled. She had been sure that Jade would argue with her. *Maybe Jade is just tired of saving my butt.* With the hard and not-so-hard parts over, it was time to mentally prepare for the next one—the tooth.

Anna and Jade sat in the tree, watching Charlotte and her mom go about their nightly routine. They had already eaten supper and watched a little television together. The orange cat was always by the girl's side or on her lap. If the cat went to bed with her, that could make Anna's plan trickier as cats loved to chase after small, moving items. Usually, those items were little balls, feathers, yarn, and mice, but a moving tooth might also get the cat's attention.

Soon, the show ended, and Charlotte's mom turned off the screen. Charlotte walked to the bathroom, Mr. Cat following, to brush her teeth and put on her pajamas for bed. Her mom followed her to her room to tuck her in, kiss her forehead, and tell her how much she loved her before turning off the light and closing her bedroom door. Charlotte had a pink unicorn night light, and it was just enough for Anna to see where Charlotte slept on the bed. Anna lucked out. The cat had decided to sleep at Charlotte's feet and not near the pillow where he might've felt movement.

Anna rubbed her hands together as if warming them up would help her magic warm up too. She knew her trainer didn't like her using her wand, but she pulled it out of her pocket anyway. This was the first time implementing her plan, and she didn't want to risk it going wrong. She flew from the branch to stand on the window ledge just outside Charlotte's room. The pillow end of the bed was right in front of her now.

The first step was one of the traditional ones. She pointed the wand at the glass in front of her and made a circle of it invisible. This would let her step through the window if she needed to, but for her plan, she shouldn't. Through the opening, she pointed her wand towards the pillow, around where the tooth would be, and released a magic tether. Children usually enjoyed putting it right in the middle, thinking it would make the tooth easier for their fairy to find.

Anna felt her tether catch the tooth and started pulling it towards her. She couldn't help but hold her breath as if breathing would make her lose concentration. As the tooth reached the window, Anna moved to the side and floated it through the hole. She lowered the tooth to the sill and returned the window to normal. Then, she shrank the tooth to put it into her tote bag.

"That's it?" Jade asked. "Just take the tooth and not leave the coins is your new idea?"

"Nope," Anna said as she flew passed Jade towards a different window...

Chapter Six

JADE FOLLOWED ANNA AS she flew for the windowsill outside the living room and kitchen area. This was the window Anna had watched Charlotte through as she had gotten ready for school that morning.

"You definitely have me curious," Jade told her. Anna smiled at her and pulled the little drawstring bag out of her tote. Inside were five gold coins, known to humans as dollar coins, and a little drawing of a tooth with wings on it that Anna had also included. She sat the bag down on the ledge and used her magic to grow it, the coins, and the picture to human-size. She shook her arms out and closed her eyes to relieve some nervousness. Then, just like in her bedroom, she made the entire bag disappear.

Anna turned to look inside the house towards the cat's food container. She pointed her wand towards the container and focused again. She watched as the coin bag came into view and could be seen lying inside, on top of the dry food. Anna stood up and tucked her wand back into her pocket. Making sure it was secured away, she started doing a little jig-like dance on the ledge.

Suddenly, the ledge was no longer under her feet! Quickly, she fluttered her wings before she landed on the ground below. Jade had followed her just in case she needed to catch Anna. Anna let her wings set her on the ground softly, and Jade landed next to her. “Whoops,” Anna said with a laugh. “At least my clumsiness waited until after my task was finished.”

“So. You got the tooth and then put the coins in the cat food. How is that supposed to work?” Jade asked in disbelief.

"You will just have to come back in the morning and watch with me," Anna replied. "I only thought of the action part of the plan. This is the first time actually doing it, so I have no clue what the reaction will be yet."

Jade shook her head. "Well, if that's it for now, let's both head home for some sleep and then meet back in the tree to watch. I hope your plan works," Jade told her and then flew off.

Anna flew up to Charlotte's window just to take a look at her sleeping again. Mr. Cat was still lying at the girl's feet. He opened his eyes to catch her watching. Seeing her on the other side of the window, he figured she wasn't a threat and snuggled his head into the blanket to doze back off. Anna gave a little smile. The cat was cute while sleeping—as long as she was on this side of the window.

She flew home. Of course, her parents were waiting as soon as she came through the door. "How did it go?" they asked nervously.

"We'll see," Anna told them secretively. She smiled at them and went to her room to go to bed. She prayed to the fairy gods that her plan would work out. Just like Charlotte, she brushed her teeth and put on her pajamas. She set her alarm for a little before Charlotte would wake up so she could have breakfast before going to watch her plan unfold.

It took a while for her to fall asleep, full of worry. She worried about the girl's reaction. She worried about what the Queen would think. Anna also worried about her own family's reaction to her modern ideas. When she finally did fall asleep, she continued to see their faces in her dreams.

Chapter Seven

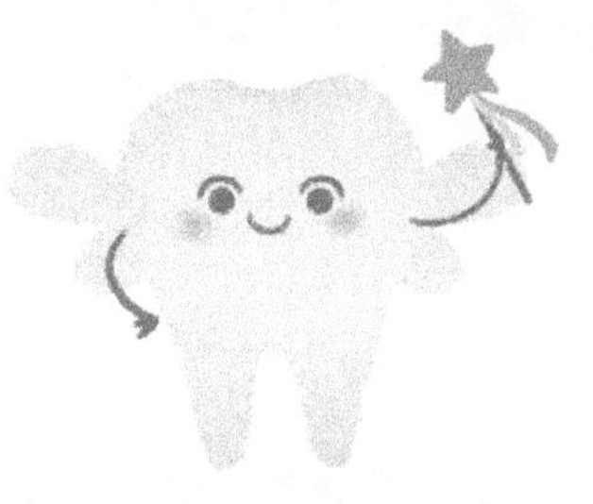

ANNA WAS JUST LANDING on the tree branch when out of nowhere, she heard, “Boo!” She took a step back and would have fallen backward if it wasn’t for Jade grabbing her hand.

“What did you do that?!” Anna shouted at her once she got her balance back.

"I'm not a morning fairy," Jade replied with a shrug. "That's why I'm a tooth fairy. We are only *supposed* to work at night, except for you making me come here. So, I needed some entertainment," she finished with a laugh.

"Well, you know I'm clumsy, and you shouldn't have done that."

"Eh, it's already done. I can't take it back. I can say I'm sorry, though."

"Thanks," Anna accepted it. She found a spot to sit as she looked through the window into the living room and kitchen again.

"Well, there's Charlotte, and she doesn't look happy," Jade said as she pointed out the obvious.

"She might be sad now, but she hasn't gotten through her routine yet." Anna pulled out her wand to make a small hole in the window so they could hear what Charlotte and her mom would say.

Charlotte wasn't talking much as she slowly ate her cereal. Her mom kept making excuses like maybe Charlotte accidentally knocked her tooth off her bed as she slept, or perhaps the tooth fairy had been too busy to come yet. Anna didn't like hearing those things since they weren't true. She knew that she just had to wait until the girl fed her cat, aware that until then, the mom was simply trying to cheer her daughter up.

Charlotte mumbled, "Maybe," as she took her bowl to the sink.

"Ready?" Anna asked Jade to get her attention. "Watch."

Charlotte shuffled her feet towards the food bin and slowly reached down to lift the lid. Mr. Cat rubbed against her ankles to give affection and gratitude for what she was about to give him, or maybe he thought it would cheer her up. Either way, as soon as the lid was lifted, Charlotte squealed with delight. Her mom came running, thinking it was a bad scream. "What's wrong, Sweetie?"

"Nothing, Mom," she answered. "My tooth fairy did come! She put the coins in the cat food," she said with a giggle. "Silly fairy."

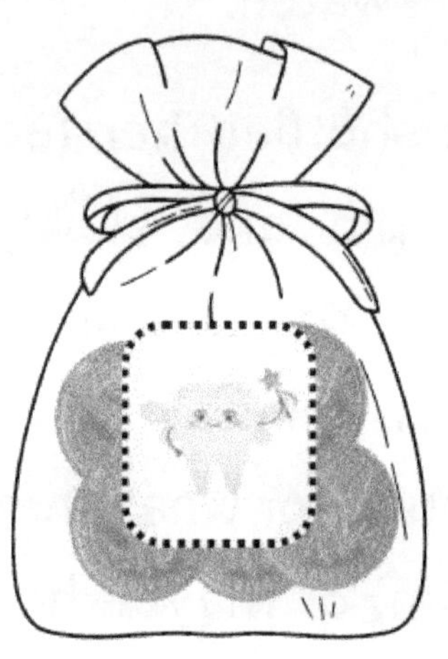

"Well, maybe your fairy noticed that you've been taking good care of your cat. Maybe this is her way of telling you good job," her mom said, smiling now that her daughter was happy again.

"I can't wait to tell my friends at school! What a sneaky tooth fairy," she said with excitement.

"Well, since your tooth fairy noticed how well you took care of your cat, maybe you should feed him quickly before your bus gets here." Her mom reminded her. Charlotte quickly gave Mr. Cat food, slid on her shoes, and grabbed her book bag. She handed her mom the coin pouch before running out the door just in time for the bus doors to open.

Anna closed the hole in the window back up and then turned to Jade. "See! She was happy and said she would tell all of her friends!"

"She might be happy, but let's hope all of her friends don't expect their tooth fairy to be sneaky," Jade replied. "I don't know if you will get assigned her friends or not, or if you will have enough notice, like with Charlotte, to see their routines. How will you handle a child with short notice?"

"All kids have a similar routine, don't they?" Anna asked. "They wake up. They eat breakfast. Then, on schooldays, they put on their shoes and grab their bags to leave. There is always someplace I can hide the coins where they'll find them."

Chapter Eight

CHARLOTTE DID INDEED GO to school and tell her friends. Those children went home to tell their parents about Charlotte's silly tooth fairy. They were excited and wondered if they would get a silly fairy or a regular fairy. All the parents could do was listen and tell them they wouldn't know what tooth fairy they would get until they lost a tooth. Each of the children said they couldn't wait to find out.

How did Anna know about this? A few of the children had their tooth fairies watching, listening. Those fairies flew back to talk to Queen Mary. They wanted to know who this silly tooth fairy was. They wanted to know what the fairy did that the children loved so much.

Word traveled fast through their community that the Queen wanted to talk to Anna. The children had mentioned Charlotte in their tales, and the Queen knew Anna had been her fairy, along with trainer Jade. *Will this be a good meeting, or will I be losing my future?*

Anna didn't know, but she knew she had to get to the Queen's quickly. Just like before, any delay could seem disrespectful to the Queen. No one wanted that, especially Anna, who wanted to keep her spot.

The guards must have been watching for her because the window into the throne room was already open for her to fly through. She glided to the window ledge and walked through the doorway. Without stopping, she kept walking until she stood in the same place she had while visiting a couple of days ago.

"Why hello, Anna," the Queen greeted.

Anna curtsied. "Your Majesty."

The Queen's smile looked happy but also uncertain. Queen Mary had never seemed unsure before, not in front of people at least. "I have heard from other fairies that you have caused quite a stir in the children's community." Anna didn't know if the Queen wanted her to speak or not, so she stayed quiet and just nodded. She wouldn't deny the rumors since they were true. "I told you that you needed to find a way to deliver the coins to the children, and you surely did. However, that was just one time. While the girl's friends seem excited about your methods, we must try it out on other children. We should be sure your way will keep working if you are to remain a tooth fairy."

"Yes, Queen Mary," Anna said. "What would you like me to do?"

"There is a young boy called Junior and a little girl named Krysta. They live in different houses, and you didn't have time this morning to research their routines. You are to be their tooth fairy tonight. Jade will go with you to watch and be there if you need her for anything."

"Yes, my Queen," Anna said. "Thank you for giving me the chance to prove myself."

Queen Mary waved her hand in dismissal. Anna gave another curtsy before flying back out the window. The last time she had a meeting, she needed to go to her quiet spot to think before going home. This time, she flew to the mushroom circle to see if her new friend was there.

She landed on her favorite mushroom, the red one with the white spots. She looked around and didn't see anyone else. Instead of just leaving, Anna decided to sit and rest. The Queen didn't want her to do any research on the children before she visited them, so Anna chose to enjoy the peace. She knew her parents would want her to tell them about the latest visit with the Queen. Sitting here, she could get her thoughts figured out before telling them anything.

Chapter Nine

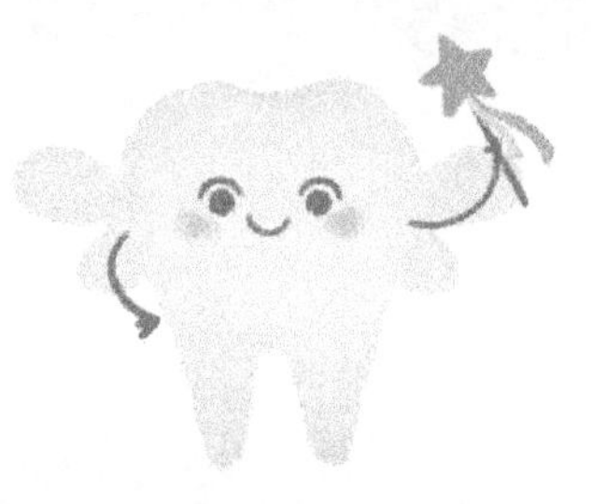

"Hey, Clumsy," Jax said as he landed on his blue mushroom.

Anna had thought he might show up. This time, she didn't almost fall off her mushroom seat. "Clumsy?" she asked.

"Well, the last time we met, I told you my name, but I never got yours. You told me you were clumsy, so that's what I have been calling you in my head."

Anna laughed. "I guess that name works. If you get tired of calling me Clumsy, my name is Anna."

"Is this the Anna I have heard that's been exciting the children about the tooth fairy? The tooth fairy that sounds like, maybe, she believes in herself?"

"You gave me some good advice. You told me to be creative, and I did. I'm just hoping that what worked for one child will work for the others. Queen Mary has me visiting two children tonight as a test."

"With how excited the children have been, I am sure your plan will continue to work."

"You know... You have had more faith in me, a stranger, than my own family," Anna told him.

"Sometimes it takes someone you don't know to see things that others have gotten used to," Jax told her.

He is right, Anna thought. Her family grew up with her clumsiness, so they just learned to expect it. No one thought to encourage her to try other things or find a way around them. They probably thought she would mess it up like she usually did.

"I have to go home," Anna said. "Want to meet back here tomorrow around the same time?"

"Sure," Jax told her. "Then you can let me know how it went."

Anna flew home. She couldn't help but think her new friend was a little cute, besides smart. She really did want to see him again tomorrow. *He sees me for me,* she thought and smiled. The thought of being able to tell someone about her small wins gave her something to look forward to. She knew he would listen without seeing her past failures. It was nice.

When she got home, the house was empty. Anna went to her room to get two coin bags ready for tonight. She drew two more flying tooth pictures to put inside the shiny bags with the coins. She practiced floating pebbles around her room for a while, then made them disappear and reappear until her mom called her down for supper. They must have gotten home while she was practicing, and she didn't hear them come in.

As they finished eating, the questions started. “How did the meeting go?” “Do you think you can do it again?” “I hope you can but if not, do you have a backup plan?”

Anna knew they would have some doubt given her clumsiness, but it still hurt when they asked if she had another plan if she failed at being a tooth fairy. All she could do was smile, finish eating, and tell them everything would be fine. She could not let their doubts get to her. *I believe in myself, and that is all that I need. Well, Jax believes in me too,* she thought as she returned to her room.

It was almost bedtime for the children, so she had to prepare.

She checked the two coin bags to ensure each one had five gold coins and a handmade drawing from her. Satisfied that they were filled correctly, Anna placed the bags into her tote bag. She opened her window and flew out—this way, she didn't need to walk past her family and hear them wish her good luck.

Chapter Ten

ANNA HAD TOLD JADE to meet her at Junior's home first. She knew that he would be getting ready for bed soon, and she hadn't watched a human boy's nighttime routine yet. Besides Junior being a boy, his father was home, and he had a dog instead of a cat. He seemed to be the opposite of Charlotte in every way. *At least dogs*

are less likely to chase fairies, Anna thought, thankfully.

She took out her wand and opened a small hole in the window that looked into the living room. Junior was watching the big screen with his father on the couch. “Well, son, show’s over. Time for bed,” the dad said as he stood up to stretch.

“Do I have to? Can’t I stay up and wait for Mom?” Junior asked.

“Mom has a late night at work. You have school tomorrow. Maybe you will see her for breakfast,” his father said, trying to remove the sad look on Junior’s face.

“Alright,” Junior mumbled. He slowly stood up and went to the bathroom.

When he was finished there, he returned to the living room and hugged his father. Then, he called for his dog to follow him to bed. "Come on, Buddy, let's go." Buddy, who looked like a beagle, followed Junior to his bed with his tail wagging the whole way.

Anna closed the hole in the living room window, then made another in a window to the boy's room. Junior lay in bed, and Buddy hopped up to snuggle next to him. Junior wrapped his arms around Buddy like he would hold a teddy bear, and they fell asleep together.

Since Anna had to make two deliveries that night, she couldn't waste any time watching the boy and his dog sleep. They were cute together, though. *At least he has the dog,* Anna thought. *Buddy was good for cuddles when he missed his mom.*

She quickly floated the tooth out from under his pillow. Buddy never moved, so she must not have shaken the pillow too much. *I'm improving,* she thought happily. Next up? Placing the coins. Anna didn't have time to see if Junior took care of Buddy and fed him or not, so she couldn't do the same thing she did for Charlotte. Then she remembered. She had told Jade that all children put on shoes and grabbed their bags before leaving in the morning, perfect!

Anna closed the hole in the bedroom window and flew back to the living room window. This family's living room was next to the entryway. The entryway had a bench with the family's shoes underneath and hooks for bags and coats on the wall. She could see the boy's shoes, the smallest ones, and his bag from her spot at the window. She created a hole in the window. For Charlotte, she made the coins disappear and reappear in a clear bin. Anna was able to see into the bin for that magic to work. The shoes were not see-through, so she would have to try something different for this one.

Anna flew up to Junior's parents' bedroom window and ensured his dad was asleep. She didn't want to risk him walking in on her and being seen or, with coins, heard. A loud snore made her stumble a bit. *I wasn't expecting that, but now I know he's definitely asleep,* she thought with a giggle.

She flew back down to the hole in the living room window once again. Anna pulled the coin bag out of her tote. She placed it on the ledge on the other side of the glass and grew it to human size. She closed her eyes to focus and then reopened them. Then, Anna created a magic tether from her wand to float the coin bag across the room. She was glad she had practiced in her room with different weights because the coins were heavy. It took a lot of focus and strength to hold her wand steady as she slowly floated them over to the shoes. When the bag was hovering just over Junior's right tennis shoe, she released the tether and let it drop into the empty heel. Then she wiped the sweat from her forehead and closed up the hole in the window.

She turned to Jade, "One down, one to go."

When they arrived at Krysta's home, everyone was already sleeping. The only animal she had was a betta fish who lived in her room. This made getting the tooth much easier since she didn't have to be as careful with the pillow or risk waking a pet. Krysta's shoes were on a mat in the kitchen, right next to the front door. This time, Anna used the kitchen window to place the coin bag through, grew it, and then floated them over to her shoes in the same way she had hidden Junior's coins. If it worked for one, hopefully, it would work for both.

As she closed up the window, Jade joined her on the ledge. "Ready to get some sleep and check back in the morning?"

"If they wake up at the same time, we should probably split up," Anna said. "I'll go to Junior's while you return to Krysta's house?"

"Sounds like a plan," Jade said. "Let's meet outside the Queen's tree so you can tell me about Junior's reaction. Then I can go to tell the Queen about both."

Anna gave Jade a nod and flew home to her own bed, remembering to set her alarm. Lying there, she couldn't help but wonder what sleeping with a cuddlyn animal to cuddle would be like...

Chapter Eleven

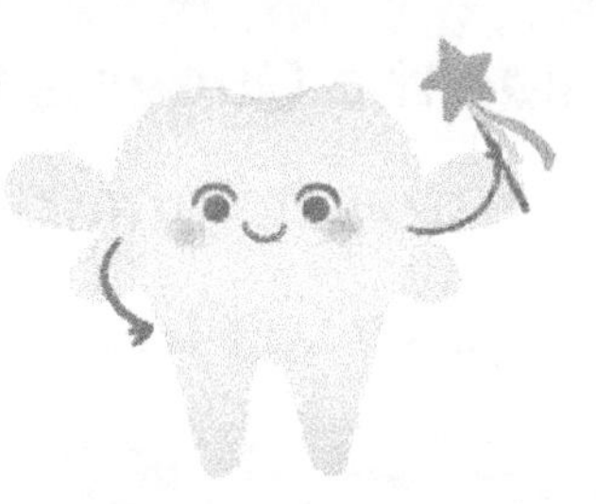

AFTER THEY CHECKED IN on the children, Anna and Jade met on the ground near the Queen's tree. Their stories were similar. Both children woke up and seemed sad. Then, as they went to put on their shoes, the children discovered the coins just inside. They both found her little flying tooth drawing and laughed. Both children left for school and couldn't wait to tell their friends.

"It looks like your plan works," Jade said. "I'll let the Queen know. Why don't you stay here and wait?"

Since she didn't have anything else to do, Anna agreed to stay. She sat down on a rock to wait. She couldn't help but let her mind wander, making up stories. In one, the Queen told her she was no longer a tooth fairy, and her family kicked her out of their house. In another, she was granted tooth fairy status but made fun of for not being traditional. She didn't know which would be worse.

"The Queen wants to see you," Jade said, stopping Anna's mind from making more stories. "Let's go."

"You're coming with me?" Anna asked.

"Of course! I wouldn't miss this meeting for the world," Jade said, excited.

Anna couldn't help but think that Jade would only be excited if she didn't have to follow Anna around anymore. *Why else would she be this happy?*

They quickly flew up to the Queen's throne room window and walked inside. As they neared the throne, Anna and Jade curtsied and waited for the Queen to speak. "Welcome back, girls," Queen Mary said. They stood up and waited patiently for the Queen to continue. "Anna, you have surprised me with your determination and creativity this week. You couldn't use the traditional tooth fairy methods, so you came up with something modern that the children loved. I have decided your fate early."

Anna gulped. Early could be good or bad for her. "I am ready to hear your decision, My Queen."

Queen Mary whispered to the guard next to her. He walked over to a door that led into the rest of the tree. He opened it, and in walked her family, along with over ten other tooth fairies. Anna got nervous. She didn't like being the center of attention or in front of crowds.

The Queen stood up and waved them all towards the middle of the room. “Welcome, everyone,” she began. “I don’t think I can remember a day when I have decided a fairy’s fate early. However, this week has not been like any other week I’ve ever had. Let this day go down in our history. I proclaim Anna as an official tooth fairy. She is also to become a trainer for any fairy who wishes to learn the modern ways instead of the traditional ones. Congratulations, Anna,” Queen Mary finished with a smile. The entire room began to clap as Anna’s family surrounded her in a huge hug.

As her family fell back, the Queen herself stepped up to Anna. "I wanted to shake your hand and give you my congratulations, face-to-face. You have made countless children more excited for a tooth fairy visit. For that, the whole community is thankful. Whether Clumsy Anna or Silly Fairy, you are now known as Creative Anna the Trainer."

From that day on, Anna was very busy. She was the official tooth fairy for the entire area where those first three kids and all their friends lived. She also used those homes to help train the other fairies who wished to learn how she did it. She would show them one night, have them practice their magic at home as she had, and then they would take care of the next child that lost their tooth.

Thinking back to last week, Anna had been afraid she would let her family down. Then, she met her new friend Jax. He inspired her to be creative. Now? She was the most popular tooth fairy and trainer in the glade. No one could have seen that coming. Not even the Queen. Yet, here she was. Happy and no longer clumsy.

As for Jax? He was still inventing new gardening tools. Anna and Jax met up every other day at their favorite spot. He would talk about his inventions. She would talk about the last child she had visited or her fairies-in-training. And their friendship grew, day by day.

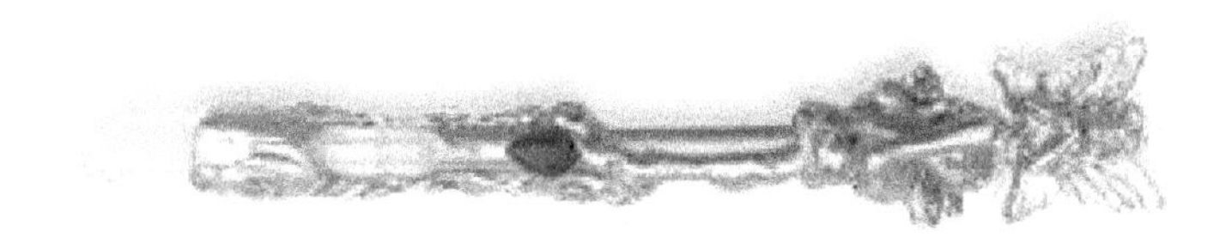

The End

About the Author

Lauren Hanson

Lauren Hanson is a writer and stay-at-home mom of three kids. She lives with her husband and children on a family dairy farm in Southwestern Wisconsin. Besides cows, they also have 4-H rabbits, several outside cats, and two dogs.

Sign up for the Order of the Quill Authors newsletter to get updates on new releases: https://www.AuthorsOfTheQuill.com

Also, follow Lauren on Facebook: @AuthorLaurenHanson

Lightning Source UK Ltd.
Milton Keynes UK
UKHW010644210922
409198UK00001B/226